SCOOBY-DOO!
AND THE
MUMMY'S CURSE

Look for the **Scooby-Doo Mysteries**
Collect them all!

SCOOBY-DOO! AND THE MUMMY'S CURSE

Written by
James Gelsey

WORLDWIDE PUBLISHING™

First published in 1998 by Scholastic Inc., 555 Broadway
New York, NY 10112, USA
This Edition published in 2000 by BBC Worldwide Ltd
Woodlands, 80 Wood Lane, London, W12 0TT
Text, design and illustrations © 1998 Warner Bros.
4000 Warner Boulevard
Burbank, California 91522-1704, USA
ISBN 0 563 47563 3

BBCB 0015

For Shira

"Hoo-ray for Hollywood!" Shaggy sang in the back of the Mystery Machine. "Like, I can't believe we're actually here!" He and Scooby had their noses pressed to the windows of the van. They were looking for movie stars.

Fred drove the van down Sunset Boulevard. He was trying to dodge sightseers who were too busy taking pictures of celebrities to look where they were going.

"Sunset Boulevard is the most famous street in Hollywood," Velma read from a guidebook.

"I can believe that," Fred said as he drove. "There is tonnes of traffic."

Daphne checked the name of the movie studio written on a letter. "We're looking for Bluster Studio," she reported.

"Daphne, like, how cool is your uncle for getting us passes to watch a movie being made?" Shaggy asked.

"Very cool, Shaggy," Daphne replied. "He's good friends with the director, Bib Humphries."

"What kind of a movie are they making?" Velma asked.

"It's about an Egyptian princess," Daphne answered. "It's called *The Sands of Cairo*."

"There it is," Fred said. "Next stop, Bluster Studio."

"Hey, Scooby-Doo," Shaggy said, "maybe we'll be discovered and they'll make us movie stars."

"Roovie stars?" Scooby asked with a smile.

"Yeah," Shaggy said.

"And they'll put your paw prints in cement in front of Mann's Chinese Cinema."

"Considering how much you two love to eat," Velma added, "Mann's Chinese restaurant would be more like it."

"Well, gang, here we are," Fred said. He steered the Mystery Machine up to a huge iron gate. The words BLUSTER STUDIO were written on the gate in tall red letters. A security guard stepped out of the gatehouse and walked up to the van. Fred rolled down his window, and said, "Good afternoon."

The guard looked over the top of his dark sunglasses. "How can I help you young people?" he asked in a serious voice.

"We're here to visit the set of *The Sands of Cairo*," Daphne said. She passed the letter in her hand to Velma, who gave it to Fred, who gave it to the guard. The guard read the letter carefully. His mood suddenly changed.

"Welcome to Bluster Studio," he said with a smile. "Go straight up this road here and turn right at the first stop sign. Park in any of the spaces painted yellow."

The guard waved as the iron gate slowly swung open. Inside the gate, Fred drove the Mystery Machine between two huge white buildings bigger than football pitches. He turned at the stop sign and pulled up in front of another enormous white building. The gang piled out of the van.

"Hey, Scooby," Shaggy said, "look over there." He pointed to four actors walking down the road. Two were dressed in bathing suits and carried surfboards. The other two were wearing khaki safari jackets and pith helmets.

Two actors dressed in a camel costume crossed in front of them and entered the building.

"This must be the place," Velma said.

"Okay, Hollywood," Shaggy said. "Get ready to meet your newest stars." Shaggy and Scooby-Doo both put on dark sunglasses and walked through the door.

"Why are you wearing sunglasses to go inside?" Fred asked.

"Like, get with it, Fred," Shaggy explained. "Everyone knows that movie stars always wear sunglasses. It's so they're not blinded by the flashes on their fans' cameras."

"Now, remember, you two," Daphne said to Shaggy and Scooby, "we're guests here."

"Don't worry, Daphne," Shaggy said. "I won't let Scooby-Doo out of my sight. Right,

Scooby?" Shaggy looked around but there was no sign of Scooby-Doo. "Scooby?"

Scooby poked his head out from behind a pole and giggled.

"Very funny, Scoob," Shaggy said. "Besides, Daphne," he added, "what could possibly go wrong?"

Chapter 2

When the gang walked into the studio building, they felt as if they had travelled back in time. It was like they were in ancient Egypt! Right in front of them was a giant Sphinx and a creepy old tomb. There were two life-size palm trees, camels, tents and statues of Egyptian gods all around. It even felt as hot as the desert.

Actors dressed in tunics and golden-laced robes were rehearsing their lines. Scooby-Doo lowered his glasses to see better. Off to the left of the movie set he saw a wall

7

of doors with gold stars on them. On the right of the movie set was a big double door with a long table next to it.

On the movie set they saw a man sitting on a golden throne. Three actors dressed as servants were fanning him and feeding him grapes.

"Now that's what I call the good life," Shaggy sighed.

"Except if you're a servant," Velma said.

A couple of actors walked by eating some doughnuts. Scooby's eyes lit up.

"Roughnuts?" he asked.

Shaggy turned. "Like, where in ancient Egypt can you get doughnuts?"

One of the actors pointed to the long table off to the right of the movie set.

"Let's go find Mr. Humphries," Daphne said. Fred, Daphne and Velma headed towards the movie set while Shaggy and Scooby went in search of doughnuts.

Shaggy and Scooby-Doo found doughnuts and much more on the long lunch table. The table was filled with plates of sandwiches, boxes of doughnuts and biscuits, lots of fruits and vegetables, and huge buckets of bottled water, juice and fizzy drinks.

"Look at this, Scooby-Doo," Shaggy said. "They must've known we were coming." He picked up a turkey sandwich in one hand and a roast beef sandwich in the other. Scooby-Doo chose a sandwich, too.

"You know, Scoob," Shaggy said, "there's no business like show business."

"Except at this studio," came a voice from behind them. Shaggy and Scooby turned and saw a man dressed in a pink shirt and blue trousers. "Here, show business is nothing but business," he continued.

"Bluster Studio doesn't know what good quality means."

"Well, they sure know their roast beef," Shaggy said.

"I'm talking about motion pictures," the man said. "Like this movie, *The Sands of Cairo*. The head of the studio hired a terrible actress, and keeps asking for script rewrites. The head of this studio has no respect for good writing."

"Like, why's it so important to you?" Shaggy asked as he grabbed a sandwich.

"Because," the man said, "I wrote the movie. I'm Azzi Fazeh." He held out his hand.

Shaggy shook Azzi's hand, getting ketchup all over it. "I'm Shaggy, and this is Scooby-Doo."

"Pleased to meet you both," Azzi said. Scooby licked the ketchup off Azzi's hand.

"Fazeh!" someone bellowed. An overweight man in a three-piece suit waddled

towards them. He was chewing on a cigar. "Why are you wasting time here instead of writing? Complaining about me again? Let me tell you something. When you've got your own studio, you can make films the way you want. Here at Bluster Studio, we do things the Rolly Bluster way. That is *my* way. And no more complaints about this picture. *The Sands of Cairo* is a masterpiece. It just needs two things. More publicity to let everyone know about the movie —"

11

"And?" Azzi interrupted.

"More rewrites! So where are they?" Rolly Bluster demanded.

Azzi handed Rolly three new script pages.

"That's more like it," Rolly said, looking over the pages.

"You always ask for rewrites but you never use them," Azzi complained.

"That's none of your concern," Rolly replied. "Now I want the camel scene rewritten. Replace the three men with an old woman. Move the scene from the tent to an oasis. I want the new scenes in one hour!"

Azzi Fazeh turned purple with rage. "Why did you hire me if you didn't want to make the movie I wrote in the first place?" he yelled. "I wish I could take this script to another studio!" Azzi stormed off.

The overweight man in the three-piece suit turned to Shaggy and Scooby. "I don't pay you guys to eat," he said to them. "Why aren't you on the set?"

"B-B-But we're not —" Shaggy began.

"Don't argue with me," he bellowed. "When Rolly Bluster says jump, you say how high!"

"Rolly *Bluster*? As in *Bluster* Studio?" Shaggy asked.

"As in the one who signs your payslip. Now get back to work!" Rolly Bluster turned and waddled away. "That's the realest-looking dog costume I've ever seen," he muttered to himself.

Chapter 3

Fred, Daphne and Velma made their way to the edge of the movie set. They were standing just off to the left side, not too far from the row of dressing room doors. Angela Belvedere, the famous movie star, was on the movie set, preparing for the next scene. She was dressed in a royal red gown and was wearing a huge emerald medallion around her neck.

A short, middle-aged woman with blonde hair stood next to Velma. She was biting her nails nervously.

"Just look at her," she said to no one in particular. "Angela looks ridiculous in that costume. She's supposed to be Princess Flora. Does she look like a Princess Flora?"

Fred, Daphne and Velma looked at one another. They weren't sure if they should answer the woman.

"You must think I'm nuts," the woman continued. "But I'm not. Just an agent. Angela's agent. I'm Cecilia Roberts."

"Hi," Daphne began. "I'm Daphne. This is Velma and Fred."

"I don't recognize you," Cecilia said. "Who are you signed with?"

"Me?" Daphne's eyes widened with surprise. "I'm not signed with anyone. I'm not an actress. We're here to see a friend of my uncle, Bib Humphries. Do you know him?"

"Bibby? What a doll. He's over there, honey." Cecilia pointed to a man looking through one of the movie cameras.

"He sure looks like a director," Velma said.

Bib was wearing jeans and a T-shirt and had on a red baseball cap. He was speaking with the cameraman.

"He's a good director, don't get me wrong," Cecilia continued, "but this movie is simply wasting Angela's talent. I'm not one of those who believes that a bad movie is better than no movie. I'd do just about anything to get her off this film."

Suddenly, Angela screamed.

Everyone turned and saw one of the huge Egyptian statues teetering back and forth. It was right next to Angela, who was so frightened she couldn't move. Slowly, the enormous statue toppled over and *CRASH!* It smashed into a million pieces, just missing the actress. Angela ran off the movie set screaming. She ran right by Cecilia, Fred, Daphne and Velma and into her dressing room. She slammed the door so hard the gold star fell to the floor.

"Don't worry, Angela!" Cecilia shouted. "I'm going to find that no-good Rolly Bluster and give him a piece of my mind! I won't stand for statues falling on you. It's not in your contract. We'll let the newspapers know what's going on here and finish off this picture!" Cecilia stormed off in search of Rolly Bluster.

Shaggy and Scooby came running over from the lunch table.

"Like, what's all the commotion?" Shaggy asked. "We heard this big crash and nearly swallowed our sandwiches whole."

"One of the statues fell over on the set," Daphne explained.

"Something seems funny about that," Velma said. "Statues don't just fall over."

"You're right, Velma," Fred said. "There's something strange going on here."

Chapter 4

*B*ib Humphries, the director, walked onto the movie set. He turned to address the cast and crew. "Okay, everybody take five," he called. The whole cast turned and left the set in a hurry. Only a few stagehands remained behind to clean up the pieces of broken statue.

Bib looked over and saw the gang standing there. Daphne stepped forward.

"Mr. Humphries, I'm Daphne Blake," she said.

"Who? Oh, Daphne, of course," Bib said,

19

smiling. "You sure picked an unlucky day to visit the set. But the way things have been going lately, I don't know if any day would be lucky."

"So, like, what's 'take five' mean?" Shaggy interrupted.

"It's movie talk," Bib said. "It means take a break. Most people usually get something to eat."

"Hey, Raggy," Scooby said.

"Yeah, buddy?"

"Ret's rake rive!" Scooby smiled broadly.

"Let's make it an even ten, buddy." Shaggy and Scooby turned to go back to the food table. "We'd better put our shades back on," Shaggy suggested. "You never know when someone's going to want to take a picture."

"Excuse me, Mr. Humphries" Velma began.

20

"Please," Bib interrupted, "everyone on the set calls me Bib."

"Well, Bib, what did you mean about the way things have been going lately?" Velma asked.

"Well," Bib sighed, "strange things have been happening."

"Like what?" Fred asked.

"Last week, a bunch of coconuts fell from one of the palm trees," Bib explained. "They nearly hit one of the actors. A few days later, one of the tents collapsed on a propman. Things like that."

"Are you sure it's not just someone playing practical jokes?" Daphne asked.

Bib shook his head. "Too many things have happened for this to be some kind of practical joke."

"Maybe there is another reason," came a voice from

behind them. It was Azzi Fazeh. He was holding a book in his left hand.

"Before I wrote *The Sands of Cairo*, I did some research," he explained. "I was looking up things about ancient Egypt when I came across this." He opened the book and showed everyone the page. It was a drawing of a beautiful medallion.

"Jinkies," Velma said. "That looks just like the medallion that Angela Belvedere was wearing."

"That's right," Azzi Fazeh confirmed. "According to a legend in this book, it belonged to a great Egyptian prince. He put a curse on the medallion. If the jewel ever left his tomb, the mummy would find the medallion

and punish whoever had it. The mummy will stop at nothing to get the jewel back."

"Wow," Daphne said. "Do you think a mummy's been doing all of these things?"

"I didn't think so at first," Azzi replied. "But now I am not so sure."

"You don't really believe in a mummy's curse, do you?" Velma asked.

"At this point," Bib said, "I don't know what to believe, except that people are in danger because of this movie."

Another scream echoed across the movie set. This time it came from Angela Belvedere's dressing room.

Chapter 5

Angela Belvedere ran out of her dressing room and into Bib's arms.

"A mummy! I just saw a mummy!" she screamed. "Where's Cecilia?"

"Take it easy, Angela," Bib said. He tried to comfort her.

"What's going on now?" Shaggy asked, running over from the lunch table with Scooby-Doo. "Like, how do you expect a person to take five with all this screaming going on?"

"Angela, darling, what is it? What's

wrong?" Cecilia called from the front door. She ran up to Angela.

"She saw the mummy," Azzi said.

"The what?" Cecilia asked.

"The mummy," Daphne repeated.

"The mummy?" Shaggy and Scooby said together.

"The mummy came into my dressing room," Angela explained. "I was resting and I opened my eyes and there he was! Then he reached down with his bandaged hands and ripped the medallion off the necklace."

"Then what happened?" Fred asked.

"I screamed, jumped up, and ran out of there as fast as I could," she said. She looked over at Cecilia. "Cecilia, get me off this film."

"Of course, Angela," Cecilia replied. "Bib, tell that Rolly Bluster he can expect to hear from me in the morning." Cecilia and Angela walked to the front door and left the building.

Daphne turned to Bib. "Gee, what are

you going to do now, Bib?" she asked.

"I don't know what I can do," he answered sadly. "With a mummy's curse and no star, I don't think we can finish this movie."

"You can and you will finish this movie!" someone bellowed. It was Rolly Bluster, waddling onto the set. "No talk of mummies or curses is going to stop a Bluster Studio production. It's all good for publicity, anyway. Understand?"

"But Mr. Bluster," Azzi said, "we've lost Angela."

"I'll worry about Angela," Rolly Bluster replied. "You worry about writing some decent lines. Now everyone get back to work!" Rolly stomped off to his office.

No one said a word until they heard the door slam behind Rolly Bluster. Then Fred stepped forwards.

"Suppose you were able to find the truth about the mummy," Fred said. "Would that help?"

"I suppose so," Bib said. "It would ease everyone's nerves and might even get Angela back."

Fred, Daphne and Velma exchanged a quick glance. "This mystery is right up our alley," Fred said. "You take care of the movie, Bib. We'll take care of this mummy."

"And Scooby and I will take care of lunch," Shaggy said. Scooby smiled and nodded his head.

"Runch!" he barked.

"But not until after we solve this mystery," Daphne said.

"Awwww," Scooby moaned.

"Let's split up and look for clues," Fred said. "Daphne and I will check out the set."

"I'll look in Angela's dressing room," Velma said. She turned and headed for the actress's dressing room.

"Great," Fred replied. "Shaggy and Scooby, you two look around on the other side of the set. Keep your eyes open for anything that might look suspicious."

"Like mummies," Daphne added.

"How about daddies?" Shaggy asked. "Get it, Scoob? Mummies and daddies?"

Scooby and Shaggy laughed as they walked to the other side of the movie set.

Chapter 6

Shaggy and Scooby-Doo crossed the movie set and stood by the big double doors on the other side.

"We'll never get discovered by a famous director if we're backstage looking for clues," Shaggy said. Just then, someone carrying a huge plate filled with food walked by them and through the double doors. Shaggy's and Scooby's eyes lit up.

"Then again," Shaggy said, "there's nothing wrong with a little detective work every once in a while."

"Rrrright!" Scooby agreed. His big pink tongue swept across his lips and nose. "Ret's go."

Shaggy and Scooby followed the man carrying the food tray. They went through the double doors, down a hall, and turned right. The room was filled with more food than they had ever seen. Tables and tables of grapes, pineapples, melons, breads, nuts, cakes, sandwiches . . . and pizza!

"Well, Scooby-Doo, let's go look for clues," Shaggy said. The two of them marched into the room and started examining the plates.

Shaggy picked up a slice of pizza. "This pepperoni pizza looks very suspicious to me."

Scooby reached over and picked up a piece of cake. "Me roo," he agreed.

"We'd better make sure everything's okay."

Shaggy smiled and took a big bite of the pizza. Scooby gobbled down the piece of cake.

"Owwww!" Shaggy yelled. He looked at the pizza. His teeth hadn't even made a dent in it. "This isn't real pizza. It's plastic!"

Scooby's eyes widened as he felt the hunk of cake slowly slide down his throat. It landed in his stomach with a *THUD*.

"Ruh-roh," Scooby moaned. He rubbed his belly.

"These must be props for the movie," Shaggy said. He looked around at all the delicious-looking fake foods. "Food, food everywhere and not a crumb to eat. Oh, well," he sighed. "If we can't eat, we might as well keep looking for clues."

Shaggy and Scooby walked past the food

tables and found another room filled with all kinds of props and costumes. Off to one side, Shaggy saw a royal throne a little like the one on the movie set. He plopped himself down on the throne.

"Take five, everybody!" Shaggy called. He closed his eyes for a quick nap.

Scooby-Doo looked over at the other side of the room and saw a great big steamer trunk. He walked on over and peered inside.

"Hmmmm," Scooby said to himself. "Ret's rook!" He crawled into the trunk and nosed around. The lid closed with a *THUD!*

"Ruh-roh," he said.

The sound of the trunk lid slamming woke Shaggy with a start.

"Huh? What?" He looked to his left and saw more props. He looked to his right and saw piles of costumes and a big trunk. "Hey, Scooby-Doo, where are you?" Shaggy heard a noise come from behind the chair. He turned around on the throne and peered over the top.

But instead of Scooby-Doo, he saw the mummy!

"Whoa! Great costume, Scooby-Doo. Like, where'd you dig that up?" The mummy let out a soft moan. "Very funny, Scooby-

Doo." Shaggy turned away from the mummy and closed his eyes to continue his nap.

Scooby rumbled around inside the trunk. Then — *BOOM!* — the lid flew open. Scooby jumped out of the trunk dressed in a top hat, a tuxedo jacket, and fancy black shoes. He grabbed a cane from the trunk and did a little tap dance.

"Rea for rou, and rou for ree," he sang to the tune of "Tea for Two." Scooby then spun around and came face-to-face with the mummy!

"Rikes!" Scooby yelled. Just as the mummy reached out to grab Scooby, Scooby

jumped into the trunk and slammed the lid behind him. Shaggy awoke with a start and saw the mummy standing over the trunk. He got up and walked over to the mummy.

"Pretty good mummy costume, Scooby-Doo," he said as he patted the mummy on the back. "What other costumes are in there?" The mummy stood and watched as Shaggy opened the trunk to look for another costume. Up popped Scooby-Doo. "Look, Scoob, it's a Scooby-Doo costume. And it's so lifelike." Shaggy reached over and grabbed Scooby's head.

"Rouch!" Scooby barked.

"Scooby-Doo, it's you!" Shaggy exclaimed. "But if you're in the trunk, who's in that mummy costume behind me?"

"The mummy!" Scooby called.

"The mummy!" Shaggy yelled. "Zoinks!"

The mummy raised his arms and let out a loud moan.

Scooby jumped out of the trunk. Shaggy

jumped into Scooby's arms. He and Shaggy
ran out of the room with the mummy close
behind.

"The mummy! The mummy!" they
shouted. "The mummy's going to get us!"

Chapter 7

Shaggy and Scooby ran back onto the movie set where Fred and Daphne were still looking for clues.

"Coming through!" Shaggy called.

"What's going on?" Daphne asked.

"The mummy!" Scooby said.

"He's after us!" Shaggy added.

"Are you sure it's the mummy?" Fred asked.

"Unless it's some guy who wrapped himself in bandages because he cut himself shaving," Shaggy said.

"So there *is* a mummy," Fred said.

"Maybe there is something to this curse after all," Daphne said.

Velma came out of Angela's dressing room trailer. "Hey, guys, take a look at what I found," she called.

The gang made their way over to the trailer. Velma handed Fred some pieces of paper. "Take a look at these," she said. "I found them on the floor."

"These look like movie script pages to me," Fred said. He and Daphne read them quickly.

"It looks like a movie that takes place in the desert," Daphne said. "Probably some of Angela's scenes."

"Then why doesn't her character's name appear?" Velma asked.

"Like, maybe it's not her scene," Shaggy said.

"Or maybe it's not her script," Fred said.

Velma walked to the back of the dressing room. "What do you think of this?" she asked. She pointed to a shattered window.

Shaggy and Scooby looked through the empty pane. "Like, this window is on a permanent take five," Shaggy said.

Fred peered through and saw some broken glass outside the window. He also noticed a trail of plaster wrappers leading away from the window.

"I'd say there's a mummy, all right," Fred confirmed.

"But if he has the medallion, why won't he go away?" Daphne asked.

Velma said, "I have a hunch that whoever's behind this mystery is more interested in the movie business than the mummy business."

Fred nodded in agreement. "I think Velma's right. It's time to write a little movie script of our own. We'll call it *How to Catch a Mummy*."

Chapter 8

"Here's our plan, everybody," Fred began. "The mummy wants this film to shut down. So we'll get him to come out by pretending we're still making the movie. Daphne, you'll be the actress."

"What should I wear?" Daphne asked.

"Grab one of the costumes from Angela's dressing room," Fred replied. "Velma will run the camera, and I'll pretend to be the director."

"What about me and Scooby-Doo?" Shaggy asked.

"You two will be hiding on the movie set," Fred explained. "When the mummy shows up, you grab him."

"Sounds dangerous," Shaggy said. "We'll do it on one condition."

"What's that?" Velma asked.

"We get to play ourselves when they make this into a movie," Shaggy answered.

"Deal," Fred said.

Scooby sat down. "Rand . . ." he said.

"And what?" Daphne asked.

"Rou know," Scooby said. He crossed his paws and waited.

"All right, Scooby," Velma said, "will you do it for a part in the movie and a Scooby snack?"

Scooby thought about it for a moment. "Rokay!"

Velma took a treat from her pocket and tossed it to Scooby. He jumped up in the air and gobbled it down.

"Now let's get going," Fred said. "We don't have much time before everyone comes back from their break."

Daphne ran over to Angela's dressing room and returned dressed as an Egyptian princess. She sat down on the royal throne on the movie set. Velma and Fred walked over to the movie cameras.

"Jinkies," Velma said. "This thing looks a lot bigger up close." She examined the movie camera and finally found the "on" switch. Fred picked up a script lying on the floor, stepped back, and looked over the set.

"Places, everyone," he called.

Shaggy and Scooby each grabbed a golden headpiece and put it on. Shaggy's was blue and gold. Scooby's was more like a crown. They ran onto the set and posed like statues behind Daphne and the royal throne.

Scooby slowly raised his right paw over his head.

"What kind of statue are you, Scooby-Doo?" Shaggy whispered.

"Ratue of Riberty!" Scooby replied. The two of them giggled.

"Quiet on the set," Fred called. "Lights. Camera. Action!"

"Oh, how hot it is here in Egypt," Daphne began. She started fanning herself. "Here I am, Flora of the Nile, awaiting my prince. I hope he will visit me soon and take me away from these hot sands of Cairo."

The mummy came out from the old tomb. Stretching his arms out, he headed straight for Daphne. The mummy let out an angry moan with every step. As he got closer, Daphne stood up and slowly backed away. Just as the mummy was about to grab her, Fred yelled, "Now, fellas!"

Shaggy and Scooby sprang into action. They reached behind them and grabbed one of the tents. They threw the giant sheet up in the air and over the mummy. But instead of landing on the mummy, the sheet fell to the floor. They missed!

The mummy turned and headed right for them.

"Okay, Scooby-Doo, time for plan B," Shaggy called. As the mummy approached, Shaggy ran around behind the mummy and got down on all fours.

"Scooby-Dooby-Doo!" Scooby called, startling the mummy. Scooby put his head out and rammed right into the mummy. He pushed the mummy backward over Shaggy.

"Way to go, Scooby-Doo!" Shaggy cheered.

He scrambled to his feet and ran off the set. "We've got him!"

Scooby turned to run but couldn't move. His crown was stuck in the mummy's bandages. The mummy reached up and tried to grab Scooby.

"Raggy! Relp!" Scooby called.

"C'mon, Scooby-Doo, you can do it," Shaggy called back. "I've got a pepperoni

pizza over here with your name on it!"

"Repperoni?" Scooby asked. He suddenly got a burst of energy. Scooby gave a giant yank. His crown was still caught on the mummy's bandages, but that didn't stop Scooby from running.

"Hey, look at that!" Velma called from behind the camera.

"Like, it's like a giant top!" Shaggy exclaimed.

Sure enough, there on the movie set for all to see, the mummy was spinning like a giant top. Bib and the whole cast and crew came over to watch. With every turn, the mummy's bandages unravelled more. Scooby-Doo kept running and the mummy kept spinning, faster and faster and faster until all that was left was a giant pile of bandages and . . . a very, very dizzy Rolly Bluster!

Chapter 9

"Rolly Bluster!" Bib exclaimed. "You're the mummy? But why?"

Velma stepped forwards. "I believe this is part of the answer." She handed Bib the pages she had found in Angela's dressing room.

Bib looked at them. "These are pages from another movie script. I don't understand."

"It seems that Mr. Bluster had plans to make another mummy movie," Fred explained.

Azzi grabbed the pages from Bib. "These

are the rewrites I gave him this morning!" he exclaimed.

Fred continued, "Mr. Bluster created this whole mummy scare to build up publicity for the movie. And he figured he could make even more money on a second mummy movie."

"The script for that second movie was coming from the scenes that Azzi Fazeh was rewriting for *The Sands of Cairo*," Velma added.

"But what about Angela Belvedere?" Bib asked. "Wouldn't scaring her off hurt this movie?"

"To be very honest," Rolly said, "I didn't like her acting very much. So by getting her to quit I could get even more publicity and find a better actress."

"What tipped you off that it was Rolly?" Bib asked.

"First we thought it might have been Cecilia Roberts," Velma began. "She told us when we got here that she wanted Angela off the movie."

"But she was with us when the statue fell over," Daphne continued. "Plus, she'd never want to hurt Angela. So it couldn't be her."

"But," Fred added, "it was what Velma found in Angela's dressing room that really tipped us off."

"What did you find?" Bib asked.

"First, there were the script pages," Velma said. "Then, I noticed some broken glass outside the dressing room."

"That means that the mummy had to be inside waiting for Angela," Daphne said.

"Whoever was behind this knew secret ways to get around the studio."

"The trail of plaster wrappers was a clue that the mummy probably cut himself breaking the window to escape from Angela's dressing room the back way," Velma said.

"Real mummies don't use plasters," Fred added.

"And I would've gotten away with it if all those kids and their nosy dog hadn't gotten involved," Rolly said.

Bib turned to his assistant. "Call the police. In the meantime, keep an eye on Mr.

Bluster in the prop shop." Bib addressed the cast and crew. "Ladies and gentlemen, the filming of *The Sands of Cairo* will continue as scheduled." Everyone cheered.

Bib looked at the gang. "Thank you very much for solving this mystery. You saved the movie. I'm going to call Cecilia Roberts and try to get Angela back. I hope you'll stay as our guests to watch the filming. I want you to feel at home here."

"Like, I think Scooby-Doo already does," Shaggy said. Everyone looked over at Scooby-Doo. He was wearing an Egyptian costume and lying on the royal throne. Two actors dressed as servants were fanning Scooby-Doo and feeding him grapes.

"Looks like Scooby's been discovered after all," Daphne said.

Everyone laughed as the cast and crew gathered around the new Egyptian prince.

"Scooby-Dooby-Dooo!" Scooby cheered.

About the Author

As a boy, James Gelsey used to run home from school to watch the Scooby-Doo cartoons on television (only after finishing his homework). Today, he still enjoys watching them with his wife and daughter. He also has a real dog named Scooby who loves nothing more than a good Scooby Snack!